The Empty Pot

A Chinese Folk

written by Charlotte Guillain ✺ illustrated by Steve Dorado

 Raintree

Raintree is an imprint of Capstone Global Library Limited, a company incorporated in England and Wales
having its registered office at 7 Pilgrim Street, London, EC4V 6LB
– Registered company number: 6695582

www.raintree.co.uk
myorders@raintree.co.uk

Text © Capstone Global Library Limited 2015
The moral rights of the proprietor have been asserted.

Edited by Daniel Nunn, Rebecca Rissman, Sian Smith, and Gina Kammer
Designed by Joanna Hinton-Malivoire and Peggie Carley
Original illustrations © Capstone Global Library Ltd 2014
Illustrated by Steve Dorado
Production by Victoria Fitzgerald
Originated by Capstone Global Library Ltd
Printed and bound in China by RR Donnelley Asia

ISBN 978 1 406 28131 6 (paperback)
18 17 16 15 14
10 9 8 7 6 5 4 3 2 1

ISBN 978 1 406 28138 5 (big book)
18 17 16 15 14
10 9 8 7 6 5 4 3 2 1

British Library Cataloguing in Publication Data
A full catalogue record for this book is available from the British Library.

Characters

Cheng, a
hard-working
gardener

Emperor

Wei and the other
boys in Cheng's
village

Many years ago in China, there was an emperor who had no children. As he grew old, he needed to choose someone to take over his throne when he died.

He decided to hold a contest. He invited every boy who wanted to be emperor to the palace.

Many boys came to the palace. The emperor gave each boy one seed to plant.

"The boy who grows the biggest plant will become the next emperor," he declared.

One of the boys, a poor boy called Cheng, was a very good gardener. He always worked hard, weeding and watering his garden. Cheng took his seed home very carefully.

Cheng planted his seed in a pot and watered it every day. All the other boys in his village did the same.

But as time passed, there was no sign of Cheng's seed growing.

One day, a boy called Wei told everyone in the village that his seed was growing quickly. He boasted about how big his plant would be. Wei was sure he would be emperor because nobody else's seed was growing at all.

As time passed, all the boys
in the village started to talk
about how well their seeds were
growing. But still the seed in
Cheng's pot did not grow.

As months went by, the other boys' plants grew tall and leafy.

Still Cheng's seed did not grow.
He tried putting it in a bigger pot,
but nothing happened.

Wei laughed at Cheng and his empty pot. Cheng decided to ask his parents for advice. They simply told him that he was caring for the seed as well as he could.

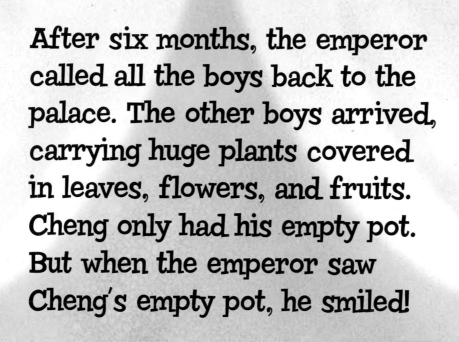

After six months, the emperor called all the boys back to the palace. The other boys arrived, carrying huge plants covered in leaves, flowers, and fruits. Cheng only had his empty pot. But when the emperor saw Cheng's empty pot, he smiled!

"The seeds I gave you had all been cooked. None of them could grow into anything!" the emperor told the other boys. "Cheng is the only honest boy among you. He shall be the next emperor!"

So Cheng and his family moved into the palace and lived happily ever after. And when Cheng grew up, he became one of the greatest emperors that China had ever seen.

The end

The moral of the story

Many traditional stories have a moral. This is a lesson you can learn from the story. The moral of this story is that it is better to be honest than to cheat. Honesty will bring real rewards.

The rigins of *The Empty Pot*

Nobody knows who first told the story of *The Empty Pot*, but the story comes from China. People used to tell stories like this for entertainment before we had television, radio, or computers. The story has been passed on by Chinese storytellers over hundreds of years, with different storytellers making their own changes to it over time. Eventually, people began to write the story down, and so it has spread around the world.